Fuck It

A collection of short stories

By Brandi Turner

Welcome to the movement!
Brandi

Copyright © 2017 by Brandi Turner

All rights reserved. This book or any portion thereof may not be reproduced or used in any manner whatsoever without the express written permission of Brandi Turner except for the use of brief quotations in a book review or scholarly journal.

Credits: Brittany Young, Editor

ISBN-13: 978-1981239733
ISBN-10: 1981239731

Atlanta, Georgia

Fuck Boy (noun)
/fék- boi/

An individual whose presence and reckless, self-centered behavior damages, annoys, angers, ruins, or compromises another individual

Synonyms: ass hole, scrub, mama's boy, trash

> In a world full of love, sex, relationships and drama, the people are represented by two separate and unequally important groups: the female who receives ill-treatment and the fuckboy who is full of shit. These are their stories...

F*ck Boy Fables — Brandi Turner

The Fuck Boy Becomes a Daddy

According to the DNA results, Roderick was the father of an 8 month old boy. Chelsey was devastated. Why? Because her boyfriend had just found out he was the father of another woman's child. The situation wouldn't be so hurtful if Roderick had told her about his "maybe son" when they first met. He'd kept that secret for the first few months, just long enough for her to fall for him. Roderick was a little shaken up by the news as well. He had gotten off the phone as soon as he broke the news to Chelsey. She didn't even get a chance to comfort him. Chelsey prided herself on being his best support system. This experience would bring them closer. They were in love and could make it work. Chelsey got in her car and took that three hour trip to be by her man's side.

When she arrived, she opened the front door and expected to see his smiling face, but the living room was empty. Chelsey walked to the bedroom.

Roderick was asleep. A sleeping woman lay in his arms and a sleeping baby lay next to them.

> "Don't make someone else's unfinished business your business."

*F*ck Boy Fables* Brandi Turner

The ImMANtation Fuck Boy

April was attempting to get over her last boyfriend. He'd taken her through some straight bull shit. April had started dating again but she still had way too many things that reminded her of her ex. He had been really good at buying gifts but it was time to get rid of that stuff, especially if it stopped her from moving forward.

April gave away the earrings and necklaces to friends and thrift stores. The best gift was a designer purse. She'd sell the purse on a consignment website. As soon as she posted the picture and description, she received a notification. April couldn't believe her luck that someone was ready to make an offer.

The message read: "This item has been removed from our site. We do not allow replicas, counterfeit items or unauthorized copies per our Prohibited Items Guidelines."

*F*ck Boy Fables* Brandi Turner

"The baggage you're still holding on to has no value and is probably fake."

*F*ck Boy Fables* Brandi Turner

The Fuck Boy's Secret

Chris had all the right characteristics of a perfect mate. Their chemistry was amazing. He was everything that Tracy could ask for after years and years of failed, hurtful and manipulative relationships. Chris and Tracy had been talking more and more about marriage, especially since the couple found out they were having a baby girl. Tracy just knew a proposal would come any day now. At Tracy's birthday party, Chris gave a long speech in front of her closest family and friends. He explained to them how much he loved her and would provide for their family. But he didn't propose. During the 4th of July picnic at Tracy's place, Chris got everyone's attention… only to announce how thankful he was that everyone was there. At the baby shower, Chris got down on one knee and vowed to be there every step of the way. But "Will you marry me?" wasn't uttered. Finally, Chris planned a beautiful dinner for the 8 month pregnant mother to be. Tracy was sure this was it. The meal was unforgettable. The atmosphere was so romantic. She could feel that this would be another moment that changed their lives forever. Chris grabbed Tracy by the hand. He began, "I love you dearly and I thought being with you would help me suppress my desires for someone of the same sex but they haven't. I have to be true to who I am if I am going to be the best father I can be."

> "It'll never be the right time for the wrong man."

11

The Unsupportive Fuck Boy

Karla and Nick had been together for over a year. The connection was great, probably because they were friends first. They both wanted the same things: marriage, children and successful careers. Unfortunately, Nick had to relocate to another state for a few months. The plan was for Karla to move once Nick got settled.

A few weeks before the move, Karla was in a car accident. Vulnerable, needy and weak were words usually absent from her vocabulary. This set back hurt physically but more so emotionally, and she needed support in this trying time. Karla would need assistance walking for a few months and she hated to ask people for help. Family took her in while she recovered. Friends spent time with her to shift her focus. Colleagues held her down at work. Nick called daily to check on her progress. However, her now fiancé, the man she had been with for over a year, the man she wanted to marry, the man she planned to move to another state to be with, the man who told her she wouldn't have to work again had not visited… not while she was in the hospital… and not once since she had gotten home. The weeks and months begin to pass as she recovered. Karla wondered what had she done so cruel that the love of her life could not visit her. She would never beg anyone for attention and she wouldn't start now. As a matter of fact, she shouldn't have to beg. Karla couldn't walk let alone drive but Nick was still too busy to visit.

> **"Adversity reveals a person's true intentions."**

The Macho Fuck Boy

Laila and Mark were engaging in a long distance situationship[1]. Mark took great pleasure in telling Laila what clothes she should wear, how she should accessorize, how she should speak to him, how she should wear her hair when they were out together and the list goes on. Laila thought Mark was such an alpha man who knew exactly what he wanted. She would do anything to prove her love to him and move from a situationship to a real relationship. Mark had his ups and downs in life and shared with Laila how he didn't have the support he needed. Laila made it her life's mission to be that support. The times they visited each other, Laila would foot most of the expenses. She'd pay for hotel stays, rental cars, plane tickets, food and gifts. Mark was still trying to find the right career fit and she was very understanding. Laila admired Mark's wisdom. One day Mark asked Laila for $500 to pay his car note for that month. He had just started a job and hadn't gotten paid yet. He vowed to repay her using his next check. Laila gladly gave him the money. She just knew this act of kindness

---

[1] A type of complicated relationship with no labels but participants engage in sexual activity.

would guarantee her a position as his number one supporter, his girlfriend and eventually his wife.

Three years passed.

Mark still hadn't paid Laila back or committed to a relationship.

> "People usually don't invest money or time into anything until they know what it is, what it does and how much it's going to cost. Relationships are no different."

F*ck Boy Fables — Brandi Turner

The Fuck Boy that Tried to Get Ahead of His Lie

Jamal was gone for another weekend. He never called when he was gone unless Alice was having fun. He didn't like when Alice had fun because it meant he couldn't keep up with her. Alice refused to spend another weekend cooped up in the house. She made a call and headed to her favorite Mexican spot with her coworker Diane. They took a cute selfie once there and Diane posted it and tagged Alice on social media. The women chatted and sipped margaritas for a few hours. The next day, Jamal finally called, but only to question Alice because he saw the picture on social media. "How do you know Diane?" "Where did y'all go?" "What did y'all discuss?" "Did she mention me?" Jamal finally admitted that years ago he had messaged Diane on a dating website but nothing happened between them. He told Alice she shouldn't pursue the matter any further.

At work the next day, Alice asked Diane to go to her dating account and find Jamal. Sure enough, the two shared a message thread… a thread that was only a month old.

> "A liar deceives no one but himself."

The Fuck Boy Who Thought He Wanted More

Jimmy wanted Kesha to take him seriously. He wanted more. He wanted her to know he loved her and wanted a relationship. Jimmy had been trying for years to lock the feisty and stubborn alpha woman down. Kesha loved him and saw his effort. She decided to take a chance since she wasn't getting any younger. Plus, she needed to give someone a try. So why not someone she had so much love for. They agreed to give the somewhat long distance relationship thing a try. On a visit to Kesha, Jimmy decided to visit family that lived in the area. The pair agreed to meet up later that night.

Kesha took the opportunity to have drinks with her bestie and catch her up on the tea. They went to their favorite spot for food, drinks and hookah. In the middle of a vibe, the bestie noticed a familiar face walk through the door. The familiar face gave a half nervous smile and stepped aside to reveal two attractive women. Behind the two women walks in Jimmy… Kesha's Jimmy. He sits down with the rest of his party and then Kesha and Jimmy lock eyes.

> "Men say one thing but their actions describe another story."

The Freely Giving Fuck Boy

Ashton and Carla had been friends for a few years. Like real platonic friends. But out of nowhere, there was this crazy energy between them and Ashton kissed Carla one drunk night. The pair soon discovered there was nothing more passionate than "we shouldn't be doing this" sex. They weren't in a relationship, just casually fucking around. She had other guys she dated and he had other girls, but they made time for one another.

Things got real for Carla when she received an abnormal yearly exam and was told she had HPV[2]. Carla didn't know if she had it since her last yearly exam nor did she know who exactly

---

[2] HPV- Human Papillomavirus is a viral infection that can be spread from one person to another person through anal, vaginal or oral sex, or through other close skin-to-skin touching during sexual activity. Most men who get HPV never develop symptoms and the infection usually goes away completely by itself. However, if HPV does not go away, it can cause genital warts or certain kinds of cancer.

STD Facts - Human papillomavirus (HPV). (2017, July 17). Retrieved from https://www.cdc.gov/std/hpv/stdfact-hpv.htm

she'd passed it to. Was she going to have to call everybody? She decided to start with Ashton. He was her friend and he would help her sort everything out and come up with a plan.

Ashton came to visit and Carla refused to have sex. She just couldn't make her mouth form the words "I have HPV." Would he be pissed? Would he call her a hoe? Would he stop being her friend with benefits or even her friend in general? Carla blurted out, "I have HPV and I don't want to give it to you if I haven't already." Ashton just looked at Carla. Carla looked at the floor. She wished he would say something and get it over with. Ashton hugged her. It was exactly what she needed and she knew he'd understand. He whispered in her ear as he pulled her closer, "The last few women I've been with have had the same thing but I read it'll go away on its own. So you're good."

> "Some gifts should remain wrapped."

*F*ck Boy Fables* Brandi Turner

The Mayweather Fuck Boy

Chris' phone was vibrating and it wouldn't stop. It was 2am. Cynthia asked Chris who was calling him and he said it was his dad. Yeah right. She already knew it was some girl that he talks to on the side. As Cynthia grabs the phone, Chris pushes her off the bed. Cynthia gets off the floor but her dignity stayed down there. She immediately starts wildly punching Chris in the face. Chris slings Cynthia on the ground, kicks her in the stomach and lays back in bed. Cynthia gets off the floor again and heaves a lamp onto his back. The glass and light bulb shatter as it hits his head. More pushing, shoving, choking, punching and then Cynthia sees red. She could have killed him. The thought of having a black eye and the embarrassment she'd face stopped her from retaliating again. Cynthia slumped to the floor and began crying from the shame. Chris kicked her and told her to shut up.

Cynthia got off the floor and went straight into the bathroom. She was praying her face didn't reveal what she had just endured. Thankfully it didn't. She got in bed beside Chris. She wanted to be comforted and left alone at the same time. Cynthia tapped Chris on the shoulder so they could talk about what had just happened. Where does the relationship go from here?

"After any kind of abuse (from either person), the relationship should go nowhere."

*F*ck Boy Fables* Brandi Turner

The Fuck Boy and the Sugar Mama

Dana was blindly in love with James. And James, well, he had a lot of love for Dana. She was ride or die and always there for him. They were in a long distance situationship but Dana was determined to get that girlfriend title one way or the other.

Dana was visiting James for the weekend. It was her first ever visit to New York. She had worked the entire summer to save up money for her plane ticket, hotel expense, rental car fees and money for food and entertainment. James always bragged about their bar scene. She was super excited to hangout with his friends too. Maybe if she got in good with them, they'd throw in a good word to James for her. James and Dana pulled up but before entering the bar, James explained that each person usually bought a round of drinks and an appetizer for everyone to share. James told her not to worry because he would be ordering for both of them. He then asked Dana to go ahead and give him her debit card to cover their tab so he wouldn't have to ask for it when the bill came.

"If you take care of the man (that's not really your man), who is he going to take care of?"

*F*ck Boy Fables* Brandi Turner

The Fuck Boy and His Secret Family

Amber met a guy through social media. A guy she had been unknowingly following for years. He messaged her, asked a few questions and said he was looking for a wife. Devonte was straightforward and dark skinned with a cute smile. Just her type. Despite living in separate states, the two managed to get to know each other quite well. After a few face times and visits, they were later a couple. Devonte was the sweetest guy Amber had dated in a while. She considered him a surprising breath of fresh air. He made her feel special while showering her with affection and gifts, and he was very sensitive. Three months after they met, Devonte had flowers delivered to Amber's job. She was so surprised that she cried. All her coworkers were just as smitten with him as she was. Devonte had been asking Amber for weeks to post pictures of them together and to tag him in stuff on social media, but Amber had refused. She didn't want to be "that girl that had a new man every five seconds." But this was the perfect time. A few likes, comments and hours later, Amber notices a comment by an unfamiliar, female non follower.

It read, "He really is a nice guy."

Amber clicked on the profile only to be directed to a page with Devonte holding the mystery woman's pregnant hand. Maternity pictures, baby shower photos and pictures of a baby girl were everywhere. Amber's heart drops. She immediately calls Devonte to demand an explanation. Devonte didn't have anything to say. He was just so disappointed in Amber's snooping.

"Before entering a relationship, post a picture of your boo on social media and if no one claims him in 30 days, proceed with caution."

*F*ck Boy Fables* Brandi Turner

The Attached Fuck Boy

Messiah had been trying to lock Lyrical down since they dated their freshman year in college. That was six long years ago. Lyrical was just down to earth, classy, driven, independent and gorgeous. Messiah had to have her no matter who she was dating or what she had going on. He made it his business to keep in touch with her. Lyrical didn't mind because they were actually friends, but Messiah made it difficult to not get annoyed. If Lyrical didn't answer his phone calls, he would call again and again. He would then leave a voicemail to say he called. Messiah would text her just in case she didn't get the voicemail. If he noticed a read receipt, he would text her that he saw she read the message and didn't respond. Messiah would proceed to message Lyrical on every social media site pouring his heart out about how they were meant to be together and should get married. To top it all off, he'd tell her to have a nice life, unfriend and block her, but request her back the next day.

Every now and then, Lyrical would respond when he asked what she was doing. Messiah would be so excited that he'd screenshot their messages and post them as if she was his bae! Messiah had a nasty habit of tagging her in pics and posting heart eyes in the comments. Just too much.

> "Persistence is not always attractive."

The Pouting Fuck Boy Gets His Way

Michelle and Sidney had been dating for a few weeks. Michelle was fresh out of a three year relationship. Her ex-boyfriend told her he was just no longer interested. Being with Sidney made her feel wanted and made her confident again, but she wasn't ready for intimacy. The furthest Michelle and Sidney had gone was probably second base but Sidney had needs. He told Michelle they were having game night at her place. The loser of any game they played would have to take shots of tequila. They played every game they could think of like Jenga, Checkers, Uno, Go Fish, Monopoly, SORRY, Tonk, Connect Four and Rock Paper Scissors. With the bottle empty things got intense. Clothes were off. Sidney puts Michelle in the air with her pussy in his face. Michelle can't take the pleasure. Sidney puts her down but as he begins to turn her around for his favorite position, he notices Michelle's wet eyes. She was scared and just wanted him to promise he wouldn't hurt her. Sidney put on his clothes and told Michelle she was ruining the mood. Then he walked to her room, got in her bed and went to sleep.

F*ck Boy Fables   Brandi Turner

Michelle fell to the floor crying. The embarrassment and the rejection overwhelmed her already fragile self-esteem. Michelle finally pulls herself together. Sidney was a good guy and he had been waiting pretty patiently. She couldn't let him get away because of her fears. Michelle walks into the bedroom and straddles Sidney so they can finish what they started.

> "If someone is not emotionally available when you need them the most, nothing else should be available to them."

*F*ck Boy Fables* Brandi Turner

The Indecent Proposal Fuck Boy

Tonya and Lamar had been broken up for all of 2 weeks. Tonya was done fighting for the so-called relationship. She still loved him, of course, and worried about his well-being. It's hard to turn those feelings off after being in a 2 year relationship. Tonya had moved out of the apartment she and Lamar shared. She had been trying to leave for months. Lamar didn't pay bills, his baby mama called at all times of the night, he paid his baby mama's bills, he couldn't post Tonya's picture on Facebook because it angered the baby mama and he spent weekends away from Tonya. She knew she wasn't a priority in his life but thought she could change all that. The longer she stayed, the more they argued. Tonya couldn't sleep at night when Lamar was there or when he was away. Sex was the only activity they could still enjoy together... well, sometimes. Lately, Lamar had been bringing home STD after STD. She had no one to talk to because they would all just tell her to just leave. That was easier said than done. Even when Tonya told Lamar she was going to leave him, his selfish behavior continued. He would sleep on the couch instead of getting in bed. He told her she wasn't woman enough to handle him and threatened to kill himself if she left.

With all of that, she still loved him and her newly found freedom was taking some time to get used to. When Lamar invited Tonya to the aquarium to see a dolphin show, she obliged. She wasn't ready to get back together but wanted to be around him and hear what he had to say.

Lamar and Tonya passed a shark feeding show and he insisted they watch it. She wasn't interested. The dolphin show was about to start in a few minutes and she wanted a good seat. The presenter for the shark show asked for questions from the audience and Lamar stopped Tonya from walking off, and actually raised his hand to ask a stupid question. The instructor invited them both down as soon as he finished the question. Tonya thought nothing of it. She enjoyed being the center of attention so she got excited.

The presenter gave her a tape measurer and asked her to walk backwards.

The presenter: "How many feet is that?"

Tonya: "18 feet."

The presenter: "That's my question, now Lamar has one to ask you."

Tonya turned around and on one knee was Lamar.

> "Rings symbolize commitment. Be careful what the person is committed to being for you and to you."

F*ck Boy Fables — Brandi Turner

Mi Fuck Boy Casa es Su Casa

Briana was going out of town to visit her best friend for homecoming. Her boyfriend Eric didn't live with her permanently but paid bills at her apartment and stayed when he was in town. He visited the weekend Briana was out of town for homecoming and was going to invite a few friends over to pregame before they went out. No big deal.

A few weeks later, Briana and her friends were nursing hangovers at her place. There's a knock on the apartment door. The girls were confused because it was 3 or 4 in the morning. Briana opens the door and five girls were standing there. The one in the middle asks for Eric. Briana says he's not here right now. She thinks 'why the hell is this girl asking for him at my apartment.' The visitor states they were all there two weeks ago with Eric drinking and listening to music and she had stayed the night. She just assumed he'd be there again tonight. Briana invites the group in and asks the visitor to call Eric. He doesn't answer. Briana gives the visitor her number and instructs her to call whenever Eric called her the following morning.

They were going to be on three way without his knowledge. The next morning, the plan was put into motion. Eric and the visitor held a casual convo while Briana listened and drove to Eric's house. She walks in with the phone to her ear. He says hey babe. She unmutes her phone and says Hey. He freezes.

"Sometimes the other woman speaks the truth. Be quiet long enough to listen for yourself."

*F*ck Boy Fables* Brandi Turner

The Fuck Boy That Got Over

Zion and Arnold had been living together for over 6 months… six months too long. He did not help with the rent, bills, or groceries. He was rarely home on the weekends. Arnold refused to change his ways but he didn't want to lose Zion as a lover and more so as the sole provider. Of course he wasn't about to move out. Where would he go? Their current town house was in both their names and they could not break the lease. Zion threatened to kick him out, but he swore he'd call the police. Zion decided to move out while Arnold was at work. She wanted to beat him to moving out because all of the furniture and electronics belonged to her. Arnold was low down enough to claim them as his and take them. Even with Zion's sudden departure, Arnold agreed to stay in the town house until the lease was up. The two went their separate ways and never discussed the situation again.

A few months later, Zion got a call from a bill collector. The company wanted to collect a debt from the town home she lived in with Arnold. Apparently, he had abandoned the place and now owed $3,600. The company had been trying to contact both of them. If the debt was not paid in a few weeks, it would go on both their credits. Zion tried to get in touch with Arnold but all his numbers were different. The debt collectors didn't seem too enthusiastic to try and contact him either. Zion had just gotten a big check at work and decided to just pay off the collectors. She couldn't bare to ruin her credit because of Arnold's selfishness.

> "The best lessons are the bought ones."

The Fuck Boy Valentine

Charles had given Destiny a promise ring a week before Valentine's Day. Two days before Valentine's Day, Charles left to visit his kids. He assured Destiny that he'd be back home Saturday evening so they could spend Sunday together for Valentine's Day. Destiny decided to go visit her own family. Saturday evening, she headed back to their love nest. When she called Charles to see if he was on his way too, he didn't pick up. She called again and he said he was on his way home. It usually took him about two hours so they should arrive around the same time. Destiny gets home, straightens up, cleans herself up and puts on something he'd like to take off. An hour passes. Maybe there's traffic she thinks. Another hour passes. Now she's worried and scared. She calls his phone and it goes straight to voicemail. Another hour passes. She hears a noise downstairs. She runs down but nothing. At this point she's way too anxious for his arrival. A few glasses of wine will help her relax.

Charles finally shows up around 6 o'clock in the evening the next day. Six o'clock on Valentine's Day.

F*ck Boy Fables Brandi Turner

> "Absence makes the heart grow suspicious."

The Omitting Fuck Boy

Rashawn told Janea he was going to have a few drinks over his homeboy's house. She stepped out the bathroom shortly after he left and realized his beers were still on the counter. Janea throws on sweats and runs to the parking lot. Rashawn's car was there but she didn't see him. She calls his name and faintly hears his voice. Janea walks down the stairs, through the parking lot and breaks into a sprint to the front side of the building. Rashawn was standing in front of an apartment door, which wouldn't be so bad if the bitch he use to fuck didn't live on the other side of that door. The entire pack of beer fly through the air. Janea pushes past Rashawn into the apartment. She looks under the bed, behind the shower curtain and in all the closets.

Rashawn screams for Janea to calm down. He tells her the girl isn't there. Her brother, his homeboy, lives there too. Rashwan didn't tell Janea cuz he knew she would trip.

F*ck Boy Fables   Brandi Turner

> **"Actual love wouldn't want you to trip."**

F*ck Boy Fables — Brandi Turner

The First Love Fuck Boy

Kylie and her best friend Tasha were looking great and they knew it. Their main goal was to go to their high school reunion and stunt on everybody. Kylie's first love, Lamar, was there with his pregnant girlfriend. Kylie and Lamar had kept in touch over the years. They had been boyfriend and girlfriend in most of middle and high school. Lamar was also Kylie's first. They had one of those infatuations that was hard to shake because of just too much history.

But Kylie had no problem moving on. Neither one of them had a problem. Kylie's issue came when Lamar walked past her and did not speak. Walked right pass her like they had not just talked a week ago about the reunion. How dare he act like she didn't exist?! So what if his girlfriend was there. They were friends first! It was all good… all good until Lamar texted her a few hours later to see where she was staying in town and if they could get together for drinks.

> "If you ignore me now, don't get mad when I ignore you later."

*F*ck Boy Fables* Brandi Turner

The Fuck Boy Who Loved Jewelry

Ryan was really good at gift giving. He always gave Stacy jewelry. It might be a watch, bracelet, ring, or earrings. He really loved to snag her a necklace on those special holidays. On their 6 month anniversary, Ryan got Stacy a silver necklace with an infinity pendant that housed a turquoise blue stone loosely moving in the middle. The necklace matched the earrings he had gotten her for her birthday.

Ryan had a baby mama. A sneaky one. So every now and then, Stacy would snoop on her page. The two weren't friends but the baby mama would conveniently unblock Stacy long enough to reveal some bull shit. The page was unlocked so Stacy made her rounds. She noticed the same silver infinity necklace with a turquoise blue pendant around the baby mama's neck. Stacy checked her jewelry box but the necklace was still there. Of course she confronted Ryan who responded with, "I don't pay attention to what that girl wear, and why are you snooping on her page anyway?" Stacy assumes maybe it was just a coincidence.

F*ck Boy Fables   Brandi Turner

A few months later for Valentine's, Ryan picks up Stacy a silver heart necklace with multiple hearts in the middle. Suspicious, Stacy periodically checks social media and sure enough, the baby mama shows up wearing the same necklace.

> "Separate but equal shouldn't be applied to relationships either."

The Obsessed Fuck Boy

Kim and Daron spent a lot of time together taking walks in the park, having dinner, going to the movies and even running errands. After a few weeks of dating, Kim explained to Daron although she enjoyed his company, she didn't want things to progress any further. If he didn't want to be friends she understood. She liked him but wasn't interested in anything serious with Daron. He seemed cool with her decision and even said he wanted to remain friends.

Late that night, Daron called Kim to demand that she explain to him again what they were doing. He was obviously drunk. Daron flipped out when she said they were just friends. He cursed her out, called her a bitch, told her to go fuck her mother, that she was trash and to never call him again. The next morning, Daron called Kim on social media to apologize for tripping. He just wanted to be around her and being friends was enough. A few weeks passed for the pair and they slowed down a lot on seeing one another. Kim gets another irate phone call from Daron and he threatens to spit on her. Suddenly, she hears a banging at the door. Daron was outside trying to tear down the door. Kim begs him to leave and he does. Strangely, the next day,

Daron calls to apologize. At this point, Kim was done with the situation and blocked his number. She thought that was the end of that. Wrong! For two months, Daron called and texted from different phone numbers. When she blocked one, he would call from another. She was afraid of him showing up at her house again or seeing him out in public. She finally called the police to file a report.

"If the feelings aren't mutual abort the mission, because at a certain age you don't need any new friends."

*F*ck Boy Fables* Brandi Turner

I Do Said the Fuck Boy

Shayla was all dressed in a sexy schoolgirl outfit for Rico's Halloween party. Rico and Shayla weren't technically dating, more like fucking around. Well, they didn't fuck often because their schedules rarely permitted but he was cool people. They vibed when they were together so everything was good.

When Shayla and her home girls arrived at the party, Rico seemed really distracted. She wasn't bothered by it since he did have to entertain his guests. She got suspicious when she received a text from him saying she looked amazing and he wanted to taste what was under that skirt later. Why didn't he just tell her that since he was sitting right across the table? Shayla decided not to reply. Suddenly, Rico stands up and taps his glass with his spoon to get everyone's attention. He said he had something he wanted to ask a very special lady in his life. Shayla freezes. He couldn't be making a scene because she wouldn't respond to the text message he sent. Rico reaches out into the crowd, grabs a young lady's hand, reaches into his pocket and gets down on one knee.

> "Ask questions. This way you get to decide if you want to be present when he pops his question."

*F*ck Boy Fables* Brandi Turner

The Vibe Killer Fuck Boy

The vibe between Shante and Emmanuel was amazing. They had these day dates that involved nothing but wine, music and conversation. Emmanuel was 6' 6," 285 lbs., intelligent and well established. Shante was a petite, feisty business woman. They really enjoyed each other's company. The day date lasted all day and all night. Nothing physically happened but Shante could only imagine how mind blowing it would be. She planned to surprise him at her next visit. Shante picked up some imported cigars and showed up at Emmanuel's door with them as a gift. He showed his appreciation twice, once in bed and again in the shower.

While relaxing in bed, Emmanuel told Shante that they needed to talk. The pair had only been seeing each other for a few weeks. Shante wasn't looking for anything too serious anyway. She got off the bed and faced Emmanuel. He expressed to Shante that he wasn't ready for anything serious. His ex had rushed things by having him meet her family and planned moving in together after only a few weeks. He wasn't ready to jump back into something. Shante agreed and was glad they were on the same page. This response surprised Emmanuel so much that after Shante left that night, he never called again.

> "Where there's a secure, stable, independent woman, there's a shook fuckboy."

F*ck Boy Fables — Brandi Turner

Fuck Boy Excursions

Chanel was awakened by a phone call from a police officer at 3am Wednesday morning. Her boyfriend Keith had been pulled over for driving without car insurance. His car had been impounded and instead of taking him in, they left him at a local gas station. Chanel couldn't believe it. As a matter of fact, she was very confused. She had just put money in his account for the car insurance a few days ago. The officer gave her the address and Chanel told him she was on her way. This confused her even more because the gas station was an hour and a half from where he lived. She'd be really late for work. But he needed her. Chanel got in her car and demanded an explanation from Keith. He said he had to pick up his cousin from work late that night, and his baby needed money so he decided to meet his baby mama halfway to slide her some money and see his 2 year old daughter. Mind you, the baby mama lives over 2 hours away. It was on his way back that he got pulled over. Chanel was even more confused because Keith's cousin's job was only 15 minutes from where Keith lived. How do you turn a 30 minute trip into a 3 hour one, and bring a baby out that time of night too? Furthermore, why didn't he call his baby mama to pick him up? Chanel asked him just that. Keith said he did not want the baby out that late. Wasn't the baby already out late?

When Chanel finally reached Keith she was mentally drained, tired and worried about being late for her own job. They pull up to the car impound and Keith didn't have the money to get his car out. Chanel writes the $200 check. They kiss and head their separate ways. Despite everything, it felt good being able to be there for him. Chanel knew he didn't have that support system. Not 45 minutes later, Keith called her saying he was pulled over again. Dang! This was just not his day. But he didn't have to worry. This time, she ordered him an Uber and gave him her debit card info so he could call and pay for the insurance, something they should have done the first time. After the 3 hour drive and before returning to work, Chanel put some money in Keith's account so he could get his car out again. His job was already very upset he missed work and he was stressing, so she'd gladly take this off his plate.

> "If you don't deserve the truth, he doesn't deserve your money."

F*ck Boy Fables — Brandi Turner

The None Closer Fuck Boy

Janiya and Lee had known each other for years. They didn't keep in contact much but ran in the same circles and would occasionally run into one another. It was always a good time when they were together. The two actually kissed once. Janiya had always been somewhat attracted to Lee but especially now since he'd been getting into shape. There had been many opportunities for things to get more physical in the past but Janiya would decline. It was always the same reason… Lee would be too drunk or annoying for her to go through with it. But Janiya was still willing to fuck him under the right conditions. After a party, the time came and Janiya and Lee snuck away.

Lee: "I have to have you." Janiya: "Tell me why?"

Lee: "I can't tell if I really like you or just wanna fuck cuz I haven't had you, and this would clear things up."

Janiya decided to decline yet again.

F*ck Boy Fables   Brandi Turner

> "Close the door and move on if he doesn't realize opportunity has been knocking."

*F*ck Boy Fables* Brandi Turner

The Stunt Double Fuck Boy

Mike could talk his way out of any situation. He had the perfect excuse... "But it's for my daughter." Monica was still very supportive of Mike being a new father. Mike and Monica had met when Mike's daughter was only four months old. He reassured Monica daily that he was over his baby mama long before she gave birth. Monica believed him and his actions matched his words. So after almost a year of dating she moved in with Mike. When Mike's daughter visited, Monica basically took care of her during the entire visit. She wanted to prove she was wife material. After about two months of Mike and Monica living together, Mike's baby mama wanted to take family photos with Mike and their daughter. Monica was totally against the photos and so was Mike until his baby mama threatened to put him on child support. He obliged and begged Monica to understand by saying "It's for my daughter." The "family" took photos even though Monica disagreed and threatened to leave... She didn't leave of course. Maybe Mike wouldn't post the pictures or maybe they'd take separate pictures.

Three weeks after the photos, Monica got her answer. Mike and his baby mama both changed their cover photos to the family photo. It was a picture of them all dressed in blue and yellow. Mike's baby mama was sitting beside him. Their daughter in the baby mama's lap and an engagement ring on the baby mama's finger.

"Pictures sometimes say things that you don't want to hear but need to hear."

*F*ck Boy Fables*   Brandi Turner

The Fuck Boy Versus the Marriage Counselor

Jeff complained four months that he and Lena needed to go to a marriage counselor. Jeff and Lena were not married but were already having issues with money and trust, two major red flags. Lena finally agreed and shopped around for a marriage counselor in the area. She made sure he was a middle aged married man. This way Jeff wouldn't feel like a woman was choosing sides.

When they arrived, Jeff refused to talk even though counseling had been his suggestion. He told the counselor that Lena had all the problems. So Lena started to talk and talk and talk. Lena told the counselor how Jeff left work early every Friday to visit his son for the entire weekend. It wouldn't be bad but Jeff stayed at his baby mama's parents' house with her. Lena also revealed how Jeff refused to pay rent but gave his baby mama $200 weekly. She even told the counselor she had yeast infections monthly and was not sleeping with anyone else. The counselor stopped her and asked Jeff if he loved Lena. He responded yes, but he needed her to be lenient with things because his baby mama wouldn't let him talk to his son if he didn't play by her rules. The marriage counselor suggested that the two split. On the drive home, Jeff tells Lena:

"The session was a waste of time and you have to pay for it. The counselor is homosexual and don't understand black couple's issues. He definitely didn't give you enough advice on how to fix yourself."

> **"He who points the finger outward dare not look inward."**

*F*ck Boy Fables* Brandi Turner

The Fuck Boy Who was Always Tied Up

Adrienne and Josh were young, attractive people who worked together. Josh was Adrienne's supervisor so they would just flirt. There were days where they flirted a little more than others but nothing more. When Adrienne transferred to another building for the same company and was no longer under Josh, the flirting got serious. Adrienne would send Josh nudes and Josh would tell her what he was going to do to her. Adrienne was too ready but they couldn't get their schedules to coordinate for quality time. After three months, Josh had a Saturday available and was in the area. Adrienne told him to swing through. She had a few people over watching football. When Josh arrived, everyone was drinking, eating and having a good time. He fit right in. As the impromptu party started to wind down, Josh and Adrienne crept to her bedroom. It had been a long time coming for Adrienne and the sex with him was great.

Adrienne spent the next few days trying to figure out when they would hook up again. Once again, their schedules conflicted. A few weeks later, Josh called early in the morning before work just to check on Adrienne. He had never done that before. Josh told Adrienne he really liked her as a person and actually considered her a friend. He didn't think he could mess around with her anymore. Adrienne was stunned, in a good way. She was cool with being just Josh's friend and appreciated his honesty. Josh told Adrienne that since they were now friends, he wanted her to meet his wife.

> "He is always tied up because he already tied the knot."

*F*ck Boy Fables* Brandi Turner

The Caught Up Fuck Boy

Kareem was sound asleep all cuddled up behind Brooke. She had watched his fingers move when he typed in his passcode to his phone for two whole days and it was time to make her move. They had been together for six months, but the last two months had been hell and made her question his intentions. Once Brooke was in, she went straight to the text messages. Good morning, send me a pic, nude pics, and wyd? messages between him and his high school girlfriend. Texts sent to a random chick asking to see her pussy. Other chicks she didn't know had been asking when they were going to see him again. Brooke's blood was boiling and she couldn't take it anymore. She threw the phone on his face and told his lying, cheating ass to get his shit and get out of her apartment. Kareem grabbed his phone and mumbles, "That's what you get for snooping." Then he leaves.

> "If you have to question it even once, then you already know the answer."

The Fuck Boy Who Let It Burn

As soon as the tip entered, it burned. Felt like a fire ant was on the tip of his dick. Each stroke burned. Kiera shifted to her side and it burned. She put her ass in the air, it burned. She got on top and it burned so bad she screamed out loud. She just needed to focus and she probably needed a little more foreplay. The problem was she just wasn't wet enough.

Kiera hung in there until it was over. She and David had been together for over a year. He would come home late from spending time with his son or David would be gone all weekend running errands with him. Whenever David spent time with his baby, Keira wasn't allowed to go. She and David really needed this time together. She hated to disappoint him or worse, he'd think she was cheating. She went to the bathroom and the urine burned. It burned like she was pissing snake venom. A cold towel between her legs and sleep should do the trick. It always did the trick. She'd have to make sure they had enough foreplay next time.

> "SHE will let you know when something isn't right way before you're ready to accept it."

F*ck Boy Fables — Brandi Turner

The Lazy Fuck Boy

Lisa met Bryan through a mutual friend. The pair took pleasure in trading jokes and working out together. They were both physically attracted to each other, so they had sex way before they actually discussed a relationship or where things were heading.

Bryan had a few shortcomings but not in the bedroom. He lived with his mom and drove her car. Lisa looked passed it because Bryan was an overall nice guy and the sex was satisfying. However, the nice guy routine went south when Bryan lost his job. And he wasn't looking for another one anytime soon. It was like he was just waiting for an opportunity to happen. Their dates became less frequent but Lisa was a modern, independent woman so she understood. They went dutch[3] when they did go out or Lisa footed the bill. Bryan only wanted to work out, visit her place after 9 o'clock at night, have sex and snore. Lisa was trying to hold on and be supportive but 2 months of never seeing Bryan during daylight hours was starting to take a toll on her. She was

---

[3] Dutch-is a term that indicates that each person participating in a group activity pays for him or herself, rather than any person paying for anyone else, particularly in a restaurant bill.

tired of buying or cooking dinner and having her entertainment, after a nut, be a symphony of snores. She couldn't understand how someone lounging at home all day could be so tired. Bryan couldn't even afford to put gas in his car anymore. Lisa would go pick him up and bring him back to her place. She would ask him to do simple tasks like take out the trash or pump the gas but he would just whine and complain. Bryan even had the nerve to ask Lisa to take him to the movies.

"Don't do shit for that dick when it won't do anything for you. Only participate in the 'For that D' challenge if he is also participating in the 'For that P' challenge."

The Manipulating Fuck Boy

"Let's live together," Jake said. "It'd be great," Jake said. "We'll go half on everything and save money," Jake said. Lies... all lies. Four months had past and not once had Jake chipped in on any bills. He avoided the rent, cable bill, gas bill, electric bill and their new credit card bill that he had already maxed out. Not to mention, Jake wouldn't even buy groceries or household items. Shawn was determined this month to make Jake pull his weight. She asked for half of the rent and like clockwork, Jake didn't have it.

Shawn was frustrated. It was the same thing every month. Just when she was about to lose her mind, Jake hands her $60. It wasn't much but at least she'd be able to buy some groceries. He was trying and she made sure he knew she appreciated his efforts. Jake even wanted to get out and have a good time that weekend. Shawn really needed to unwind and it'd be great for their connection. Jake took her to a restaurant he'd heard about in the city. The spot was sexy, the people beautiful and there was even a live band. Her excitement was short lived because after dinner Jake said, "It's on you baby."

F*ck Boy Fables   Brandi Turner

> **"Ride or die for someone who'd at minimum pay for dinner."**

*F*ck Boy Fables* Brandi Turner

Married Men are Fuck Boys Too

Tina was 45 years old and finally married. She was very thankful Derrick came into her and her daughter's life. Derrick was out of town for a weekend with the boys in New Orleans. Tina's cousin and friends happen to be in the same city. Tina had stayed home to work. She got a call from Derrick who was just checking on her and checking in. He mentioned he saw her friends and family having a great time. Tina already knew he'd seen her people. They were actually waiting impatiently on the other line. Tina told Derrick to have fun and sent him kisses before she clicked back over. Her family couldn't wait to finish telling her how they were watching Derrick sit at a table with his arm around another woman. Just the 2 of them. It wasn't the first time the ladies had caught him cheating that weekend either. Tina listened to her crew but she was just happy he had the decency to go out of town this time.

> **"Your dignity is more valuable than any title."**

*F*ck Boy Fables* Brandi Turner

About the Author

I am a 27 year old first time author from Midfield, Alabama. I currently live and work as an educator in Atlanta, Georgia.

I began writing *F*ck Boy Fables* around February 2017. The idea for the book came after I got a phone call from a bill collector. My ex-boyfriend and his baby mama used my social security number to get a cable bill in my name without my permission. We had been broken up for over a year and I couldn't believe I was still dealing with stuff from that relationship (The story is actually in the book). On the way home from work, I started thinking about all the situations I'd lived through. I didn't want to write a story just about my life. So *F*ck Boy Fables* was born. I knew the title would spark attention.

I wrote my stories and listen to other women tell theirs. All of a sudden, I lost my enthusiasm. It became depressing and draining to revisit those experiences. I felt stupid and gullible and I was afraid women would be portrayed that way in the book. I didn't want to be a victim. After a few months, I finished writing but changed the angle. I would make it a release for me and many others who are afraid or ashamed to tell their story.

They must be stopped!

Welcome to the movement!

Made in the USA
Columbia, SC
02 June 2018